VOYAGER

AN ADVENTURE THROUGH SPACE

By John Gustafson

Endorsed and reviewed by Alan Harris, Ph.D., supervisor for the Earth and
Planetary Physics Group at the Jet Propulsion Laboratory, Pasadena, California

Scholastic Inc.

New York   Toronto   London   Auckland   Sydney

Copyright © 1994 by RGA Publishing Group, Inc.
Photos Courtesy of NASA and the Jet Propulsion Laboratory,
Pasadena, California.

ISBN: 0-590-45764-0

12 11 10 9 8 7 6 5 4 3 2 1   4 5 6 7 8 9/9

Printed in the U.S.A.

First Scholastic printing, December 1994   24

Designed by Dan Kuffel and Susan Shankin
Typeset by Melvin L. Harris
Illustrations by Tanya Maiboroda
Project editor: Amy Hanson

Have you ever looked through a telescope to see the stars? For years, scientists have been looking through telescopes to see the moon, the planets, and the stars. Telescopes have provided us with fascinating and important scientific information about our solar system.

But there are so many things in space that scientists have never been able to see—even with the strongest of telescopes! They needed to create something that could travel deep into space and send back scientific information that we could never discover from Earth. That special something is a spacecraft called Voyager!

Earth from space

There are nine planets in our solar system. Each of them orbits the sun. Closest to our sun is Mercury, followed by Venus, Earth, and Mars. Because these planets are close to our sun, they are called the inner planets. The planets farthest from our sun—Jupiter, Saturn, Uranus, Neptune, and Pluto—are known as the outer planets.

In the past, other spacecraft have sent information back to Earth. But Voyager's mission was the most exciting. Voyager was going where no human-made spacecraft had gone before: to those outer planets known as the "gas giants"—Jupiter, Saturn, Uranus, and Neptune.

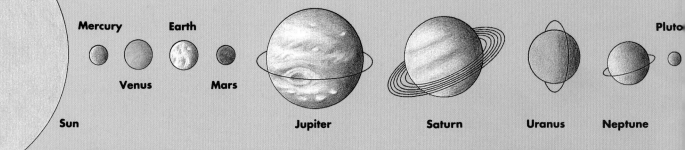

Sun   Mercury   Earth   Venus   Mars   Jupiter   Saturn   Uranus   Neptune   Pluto

How long did it take to build Voyager? Hundreds of scientists worked for five years on the spacecraft, equipping it with cameras, computers, and many other special instruments that would transmit its messages back to Earth. It had to be built to withstand billions of miles of travel through harsh radiation and the bitter cold of space.

The scientists had to schedule Voyager's lift-off around a time when Jupiter, Saturn, Uranus, and Neptune line up in their orbits so one spacecraft could pass by all of them. This is called the Grand Alignment. The Grand Alignment happens only once every 175 years!

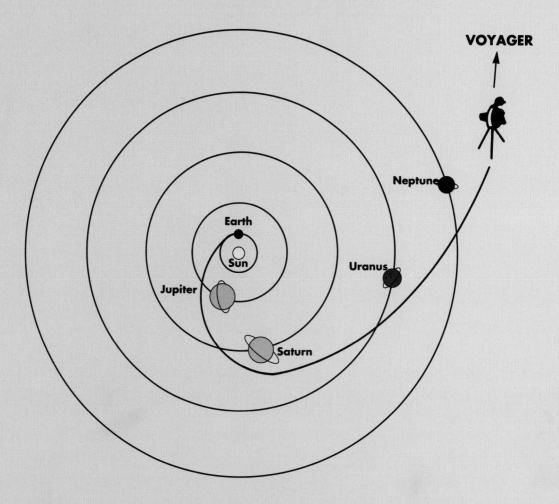

VOYAGER

Neptune

Uranus

Earth

Sun

Jupiter

Saturn

On August 20, 1977, a powerful rocket took off from Cape Canaveral in Florida, carrying Voyager into space. Less than an hour after lift-off, Voyager was released from the rocket to start its journey.

Voyager traveled 50 times faster than a jet airplane, but it still took 12 years for the craft to fly by all the gas giants in the solar system.

You don't need 12 years to reach the outer planets. Just strap yourself in and turn the page!

Nearly two years after takeoff, and after traveling more than 500 million miles, Voyager reached its first destination—Jupiter. The biggest planet in the solar system, Jupiter weighs three hundred times more than Earth. Earth weighs 13 septillion (trillion trillion) pounds (13,000,000,000,000,000,000,000,000 lbs.), so just imagine how huge Jupiter is!

While Earth is made mostly of rock, Jupiter is made up of many different gases (that's why it is called a gas giant). In fact, it has no solid surface to stand on. And because its strong winds continuously blow the gases around, Jupiter looks like it is striped.

Jupiter

Jupiter's striped clouds

Jupiter's cloud movement

A huge storm (twice the size of Earth!) has been brewing on Jupiter for centuries. It is called the Great Red Spot. But Voyager was not the first to see this spot. An English astronomer named Robert Hooke first discovered it in 1664 with the use of a telescope.

The pictures Voyager took show how the Great Red Spot swirls and mixes among smaller, neighboring storms. Scientists think that the Great Red Spot may have been formed thousands of years ago when many small storms mixed together.

The Great Red Spot

While traveling past Jupiter, Voyager took pictures of a thin ring that circles the planet. The ring is made of a band of particles that are no bigger than tiny specks of dust!

One of Io's volcanoes

The Earth has just one moon, but Jupiter has at least 16! Three of these were unknown before Voyager visited the planet. But we have known about many of the others for a very long time. Nearly 400 years ago, Galileo Galilei, an Italian astronomer, looked through his telescope and spotted Jupiter's four biggest moons—Io, Ganymede, Europa, and Callisto.

One of the most exciting pictures taken by Voyager is of volcanoes erupting on Io. Io has the only active volcanoes ever found in the solar system, other than those on Earth.

Ganymede, the largest moon in our solar system, is just a little bigger than our moon.

Ganymede

Europa, another of Jupiter's moons, is covered with a layer of ice that is many miles thick. Scientists think the ice floats upon an ocean of water that surrounds Europa's rocky center.

Callisto is also covered with ice, but its surface is marked with thousands of craters. Craters are gouged out when meteorites slam into the surface of a planet or moon. How old do scientists believe Callisto's surface to be? More than *four billion* years!

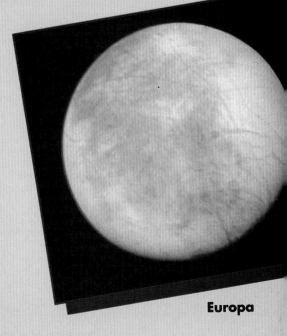

Europa

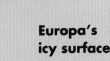

Callisto

Europa's icy surface

After sailing past Jupiter, Voyager took more than two years to reach the second biggest planet in the solar system—Saturn. This huge gas planet has 17 known moons—more than any other planet. But it is most famous for its incredible system of rings.

Saturn

Because Saturn is so far away (more than 800 million miles), astronomers on Earth normally see only a few of its features and bands through their telescopes. But Voyager traveled to within just a few thousand miles of Saturn, which enabled it to take amazing close-up pictures of the planet's atmosphere. (An atmosphere is the outer layer of gases that surrounds a planet.)

Computers on Earth then recolored these pictures of Saturn so that we could see the planet's stripes and swirling storms.

Saturn's atmosphere

Saturn with two of its moons, Tethys and Dione
Can you find Tethys's tiny shadow on Saturn?

The Voyager photos show that Saturn's rings are actually thousands of separate mini-rings. Each of the mini-rings is made up of lots and lots of icy particles, some as small as dust, others as big as houses!

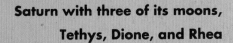

Saturn with three of its moons, Tethys, Dione, and Rhea

Titan is Saturn's largest moon. And, though scientists had seen Titan from Earth with telescopes, they were amazed to see a thick atmosphere around it. They had thought that none of the moons in our solar system had any atmosphere. The smog around Titan is so thick that the Voyager cameras could not take pictures of its surface.

Because of the haze, scientists can only guess what Titan's surface is like. Some think it might be covered with lakes or oceans of liquid methane, the same smog-producing chemical that is sometimes burned as fuel on Earth.

Titan

Titan's thick hazy atmosphere

Saturn's smallest moons are not round. One of them, Hyperion, looks like a chunk of rock left over from two larger moons that might have crashed together.

Another moon, Mimas, has a crater 80 miles across. The collision that formed this huge crater almost split the moon in two. The rest of the moon's surface has many smaller craters that make it look like a golf ball.

The strange moon Iapetus always points in the same direction as it orbits Saturn. As a result, its front edge has picked up lots of dark, dusty material and is now pitch-black. Some scientists think the dark face of Iapetus is like the front end of a car, which collects bugs and dirt as the car travels along a road.

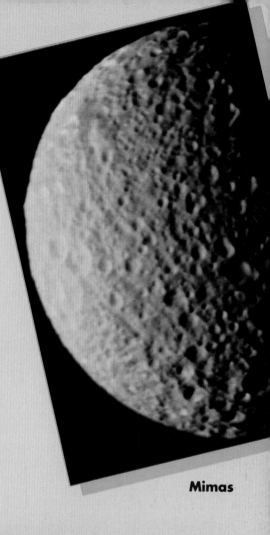

Mimas

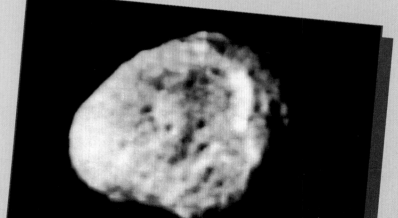

Hyperion

By the time Voyager reached Uranus, it had traveled for 8½ years across 2 billion miles of space. Like Jupiter and Saturn, Uranus is made of gas, but it is not nearly as big, and it is also much colder. Unlike Jupiter and Saturn, which have a striped appearance, Uranus looks like a smooth, blue-green marble.

Uranus is the only planet we know of that is tipped over on its side. Its eleven rings look like circles on a target.

Voyager took pictures of 10 of Uranus's 15 moons. Titania, which is covered with craters, is the largest moon of Uranus.

Ariel, which looks very similar to Titania, has many large valleys and cliffs. Some of them cross the moon's entire surface.

Miranda is sometimes called the strangest moon in the solar system because it looks as if it has been torn to pieces and then put together again.

Titania

Ariel

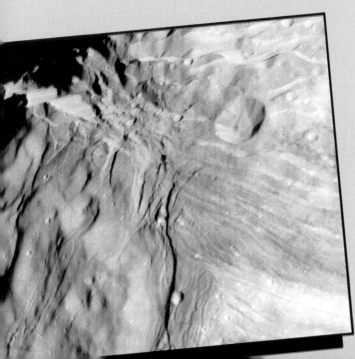

Miranda's strange surface

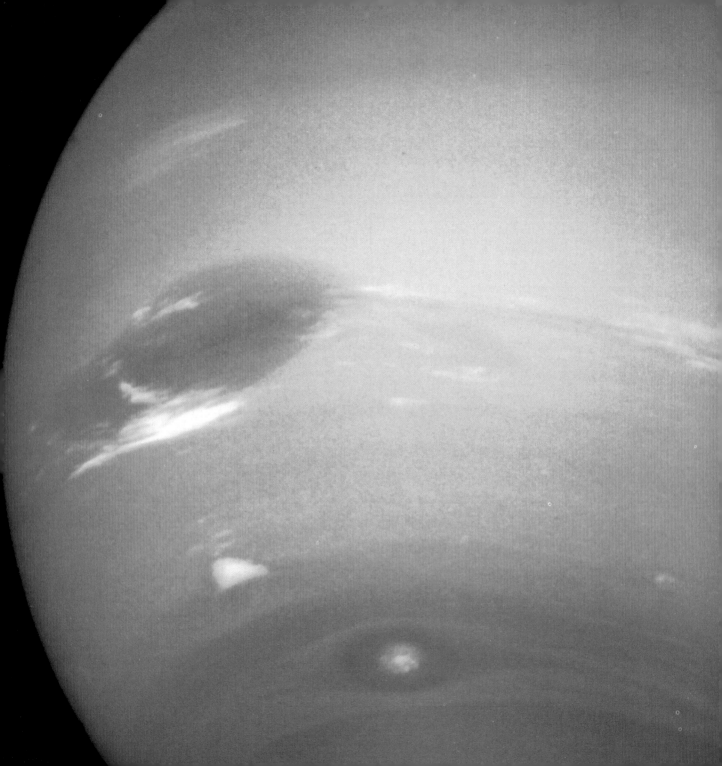

In August 1989, 12 years after leaving Earth, Voyager rushed past the final planet on its tour—Neptune. It was traveling close to a hundred times faster than a bullet shot from a rifle!

The photographs taken of Neptune show a beautiful blue planet. Neptune's remarkable blue color is caused by the methane gas in its atmosphere.

Neptune is so far away from the sun that it takes 164 Earth years for the planet to orbit the sun just once! And, the sunlight that reaches Neptune is 900 times weaker than the sunlight that reaches us on Earth.

On Neptune, Voyager discovered storms similar to those of Jupiter's Great Red Spot. Scientists call Neptune's storm the Great Dark Spot. Although it is not as huge as the Great Red Spot, the Great Dark Spot is still very big. In fact, the whole Earth could fit in it!

The Great Dark Spot

Another discovery made by Voyager was the three narrow rings and the one broad ring surrounding Neptune.

Thanks to Voyager, scientists now know that all four of the gas giants have rings.

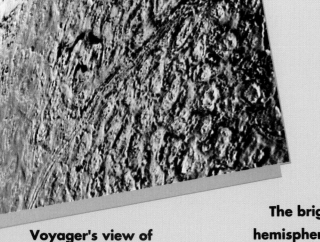

The dark spotted areas on Triton's surface may be ice geysers.

Neptune has several moons, too. Triton, its largest moon, can be seen from Earth. Scientists have known about this moon for a long time. In planning the Voyager mission, they made sure the spacecraft would take close-up pictures of Triton, which is made of rock and ice.

Voyager measured the temperature of Triton at nearly 400 degrees below zero. This makes Triton the coldest place known in our solar system.

Voyager's view of Triton from 25,000 miles away

The bright, lower hemisphere of Triton

As Voyager passed Triton, the space-craft found that the moon had geysers similar to the volcanoes on Earth. But instead of erupting molten rock like volcanoes, these erupt ice! Spray from the ice geysers spreads across Triton for nearly a hundred miles.

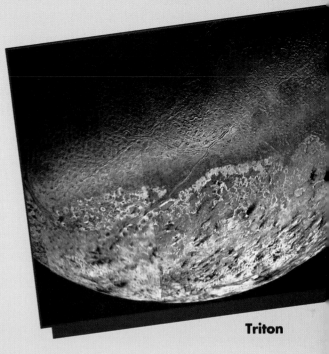

Triton

Triton's surface

After leaving Neptune and Triton, Voyager had completed the main part of its journey.

It made many wonderful discoveries along the way. Its cameras spotted moons too tiny to see from Earth. It found volcanoes and geysers erupting on other worlds. And it discovered that all the giant planets in the solar system have rings around them.

But Voyager's mission is far from over. As it leaves our solar system, it will travel deeper and deeper into outer space never to return to Earth. If one day Voyager makes its way to another star system, a special message from Earth can be found aboard the spacecraft.

Recorded onto copper and coated with gold for extra protection, the Voyager message includes people saying hello in various languages, all kinds of music, and many different pictures of people and scenes from Earth.

Scientists wore protective suits to prepare an American flag and the recorded messages that Voyager carried into space.

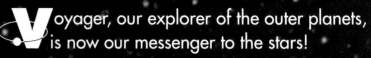**V**oyager, our explorer of the outer planets, is now our messenger to the stars!